MY BEAR
I WISH . . . DO YOU?

My Bear is an irresistible teddy bear
sure to capture the hearts of young readers
and listeners. Each page shows him engaged
in a familiar activity and is accompanied
by a rhyme that is simple, memorable, and
filled with fun. And because every rhyme
ends with a question that cries out for
an answer, here is the perfect book for
parents to read with their eager children!

D1274384

MY BEAR
I WISH . . . DO YOU?

Written by Ruth Thomson
Illustrated by Ian Beck

GALLERY BOOKS
An Imprint of W. H. Smith Publishers Inc.
112 Madison Avenue
New York City 10016

I wish I were bold
like those brave knights of old
who had banners of gold.
Do you?

I wish I could be
a fine sailor at sea
and catch lobster for me.
Do you?

I wish I could camp
with a tent and a lamp
and feel snug in the damp.
Do you?

I wish I could fly
with the birds in the sky
and watch clouds floating by.
Do you?

I wish I could glue
some bark and bamboo
to make a canoe.
Do you?

I wish I could go
down the hill to and fro
on a sled in the snow.
Do you?

I wish I could play
in the jungle all day
and scare tigers away.
Do you?

I wish, for a dare,
I could stand on a chair
with my legs in the air.
Do you?

I wish, very soon,
I could fly to the moon
and dig holes with a spoon.
Do you?

I wish I were quick
at doing a trick
with three cups and a chick.
Do you?

I wish I were king
with a robe and a ring
and a dog that could sing.
Do you?

I wish I could make
an extraordinary cake
which took no time to bake.
Do you?

First published in 1986 in Great Britain by
Conran Octopus Limited

This edition published in 1990 by Gallery Books,
an imprint of W.H. Smith Publishers, Inc.,
112 Madison Avenue, New York, New York 10016

ISBN 0-8317-6272-1

Designed by Heather Garioch

Printed in Great Britain